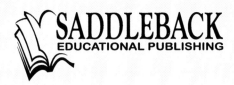

Focus ON READING

To Kill a Mockingbird

LISA MCCARTY

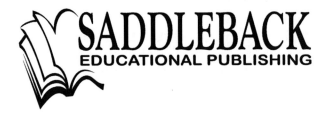

Three Watson
Irvine, CA 92618-2767
Web site: www.sdlback.com

ISBN-13: 978-1-59905-124-6
ISBN-10: 1-59905-124-9
eBook: 978-1-60291-535-0

Printed in the United States of America
10 09 08 07   9 8 7 6 5 4 3 2

Contents

WELCOME TO *FOCUS ON READING*

Focus on Reading literature study guides are designed to help all students comprehend and analyze their reading. Many teachers have grappled with the question of how to make quality literature accessible to all students. Students who are already avid readers of quality literature are motivated to read and are familiar with prereading and reading strategies. However, struggling readers frequently lack basic reading skills and are not equipped with the prior knowledge and reading strategies to thoroughly engage in the classroom literature experience.

Focus on Reading is designed to make teachers' and students' lives easier! How? By providing materials that allow all students to take part in reading quality literature. Each *Focus on Reading* study guide contains activities that focus on vocabulary and comprehension skills that students need to get the most from their reading. In addition, each section within the guide contains a before-reading **Focus Your Reading** page containing tools to ensure success: **Vocabulary Words to Know, Things to Know,** and **Questions to Think About.** These study aids will help students who may not have the prior knowledge they need to truly comprehend the reading.

USING *FOCUS ON READING*

Focus on Reading is designed to make it easy for you to meet the individual needs of students who require additional reading skills support. Each *Focus on Reading* study guide contains teacher and student support materials, reproducible student activity sheets, an end-of-book test, and an answer key.

- **Focus on the Book,** a convenient reference page for the teacher, provides a brief overview of the entire book including a synopsis, information about the setting, author data, and historical background.

- **Focus Your Knowledge,** a reference page for students, is a whole-book, prereading activity designed to activate prior knowledge and immerse students in the topic.

The study guide divides the novel into 6 manageable sections to make it easy to plan classroom time. Five activities are devoted to each section of the novel.

Before Reading

- **Focus Your Reading** consists of 3 prereading sections:

Vocabulary Words to Know lists and defines 10 vocabulary words students will encounter in their reading. Students will not have to interrupt their reading to look up, ask for, or spend a lot of time figuring out the meaning of unfamiliar words. These words are later studied in-depth within the lesson.

Things to Know identifies terms or concepts that are integral to the reading but that may not be familiar to today's students. This section is intended to "level the playing field" for those students who may not have much prior knowledge about the time period, culture, or theme of the book. It also gets students involved with the book, increasing interest before they begin reading.

Questions to Think About helps students focus on the main ideas and important details they should be looking for as they read. This activity helps give students a *purpose* for reading. The goal of these guiding questions is to build knowledge, confidence, and comfort with the topics in the reading.

During Reading

- **Build Your Vocabulary** presents the 10 unit focus words in the exact context of the book. Students are then asked to write their own definitions and sentences for the words.

- **Check Your Understanding: Multiple Choice** offers 10 multiple-choice, literal comprehension questions for each section.

- **Check Your Understanding: Short Answer** contains 10 short-answer questions based on the reading.

After Reading

- **Deepen Your Understanding** is a writing activity that extends appreciation and analysis of the book. This activity focuses on critical-thinking skills and literary analysis.

- **End-of-Book Test** contains 20 multiple-choice items covering the book. These items ask questions that require students to synthesize the information in the book and make inferences in their answers.

CLASSROOM MANAGEMENT

Focus on Reading is very flexible. It can be used by the whole class, by small groups, or by individuals. Each study guide divides the novel into 6 manageable units of study.

This literature comprehension program is simple to use. Just photocopy the lessons and distribute them at the appropriate time as students read the novel.

You may want to reproduce and discuss the **Focus Your Knowledge** page before distributing the paperbacks. This page develops and activates prior knowledge to ensure that students have a grounding in the book before beginning reading. After reading this whole-book prereading page, students are ready to dive into the book.

The **Focus Your Reading** prereading activities are the keystone of this program. They prepare students for what they are going to read, providing focus for the complex task of reading. These pages should be distributed before students actually begin reading the corresponding section of the novel. There are no questions to be answered on these pages; these are for reference and support during reading. Students may choose to take notes on these pages as they read. This will also give students a study tool for review before the **End-of-Book Test.**

The **Focus Your Reading** pages also provide an excellent bridge to home. Parents, mentors, tutors, or other involved adults can review vocabulary words with students, offer their own insights about the historical and cultural background outlined, and become familiar with the ideas students will be reading about. This can help families talk to students in a meaningful way about their reading, and it gives the adults something concrete to ask about to be sure that students are reading and understanding.

The **Build Your Vocabulary** and **Check Your Understanding: Multiple Choice** and **Short Answer** activities should be distributed when students begin reading the corresponding section of the novel. These literature guide pages are intended to help students comprehend and retain what they read; they should be available for students to refer to at any time during the reading.

Deepen Your Understanding is an optional extension activity that goes beyond literal questions about the book, asking students for their own ideas and opinions—and the reasons behind them. These postreading activities generally focus on literary analysis.

As reflected in its title, the **End-of-Book Test** is a postreading comprehension test to be completed after the entire novel has been read.

For your convenience, a clear **Answer Key** simplifies the scoring process.

Synopsis

The narrator and protagonist of the story is Scout Finch, a six-year-old girl (at the beginning of the story) who lives with her brother, Jem, and their widowed father, Atticus. The story takes place in the small Alabama town of Maycomb during the Great Depression.

Jem, Scout, and their friend Dill become fascinated with their recluse neighbor Arthur Radley, nicknamed Boo, who has not been seen outside of his house for years. The children act out the story of Boo Radley from rumors they have heard. The children find gifts in a knothole of a tree on the Radley property and imagine that Boo left them. Other incidents lead the children to believe that Boo Radley may not be the evil person the rumors suggest.

Atticus, a prominent lawyer, agrees to defend a black man named Tom Robinson, who has been unjustly accused of raping a white woman. As a result of Atticus's decision, Jem and Scout are harassed by other children, while their father faces disapproval and angry mobs. Atticus does his best to defend Tom Robinson.

Scout has faith in the goodness of the people in her community. As the novel progresses, this faith is tested by the hatred and prejudice that emerge during the trial. Scout eventually develops a more mature understanding that allows her to keep her faith in human goodness without being blind to human evil.

About the Author

Nelle Harper Lee was born in 1926 in Monroeville, Alabama. Located in southwest Alabama about halfway between Montgomery and Mobile, Monroeville is thought to be the model for Maycomb in *To Kill a Mockingbird*. The youngest of four children, Lee studied law at the University of Alabama and studied one year at Oxford University. She spent the 1950s working for Eastern Airlines and writing short stories. Her father's sudden illness forced her to divide her time between New York and Monroeville. On the suggestion of her editor, Lee developed one of her short stories into her only novel, *To Kill A Mockingbird*, published in 1960. *To Kill a Mockingbird* won the 1961 Pulitzer Prize and spent eighty weeks on the bestseller list. The novel has been translated into forty languages.

Historical Background

The setting of *To Kill a Mockingbird* is a small southern town during the early 1930s—the time of the Great Depression. One of the causes of the Great Depression was the stock market crash. From the end of World War I in 1919, the stock market prices kept rising. On October 24, 1929, the stock market crashed. Stock prices plummeted. On that one day, the value of stocks fell fourteen billion dollars. Businesses started to lay off people. Small stores closed their doors. Millions of people lost all their savings. Many people ended up sleeping in shelters for the unemployed, standing in breadlines, and eating in soup kitchens. A few people profited from the Great Depression, but most were left with little money.

Alabama was a Confederate state during the Civil War. At that time, most white residents in Alabama viewed slavery as an integral part of their economic and social systems, and they opposed attempts to abolish it. Montgomery, Alabama, was the Confederate capital until May 1861. Alabama contributed about 100,000 troops to the Confederacy, and perhaps 25% of them died during the Civil War. During the 1930s, race relations between blacks and whites were still strained and marked by prejudice. As depicted in *To Kill a Mockingbird,* there were many white people during this time who believed in and supported racial equality, but many people were still prejudiced against blacks.

It was not until the 1950s and 1960s, well after the time period for the setting of *To Kill a Mockingbird,* that civil rights efforts took off. Race relations were a major issue in Alabama in the 1950s and 1960s, as civil rights advocates worked to end racial segregation in the state.

During 1955–1956, Dr. Martin Luther King, Jr., organized a black boycott that ended racially separate seating on municipal buses in Montgomery. In 1954, the U.S. Supreme Court ruled racial segregation in public schools to be unconstitutional. In 1963, four black children were killed when a bomb exploded in their Birmingham church. The incident, widely deplored in the nation, helped to pass the federal Civil Rights Act of 1964. In 1965, the U.S. Congress passed the Voting Rights Act, which helped add many African Americans to the voting rolls in Alabama.

Focus Your Knowledge

To Kill a Mockingbird takes place in a small, rural, southern town in the 1930s. The setting of the novel is important because it affects how the characters interact with one another. The setting greatly influences the atmosphere, or background feeling, of the story.

• When you think of a small southern town during the 1930s, what comes to mind? How is the town laid out? Is there a town center? What types of buildings would you picture in town?

• Now, imagine being a child in this town during the summer. What would you do for fun? How would you occupy your days? How do you think these activities would be different from how a child might spend the summer today?

• Imagine that you are a white child in this small southern town. Are there different classes of white people? Are there black people in your neighborhood? Do you go to school with black children? Do you have black servants? What do black people think of your family?

• As you read *To Kill a Mockingbird,* you will experience the events from the perspective of a young white girl who happens to be a tomboy. What is your image of a southern lady? As you read the novel, imagine the frustration and confusion that Scout, the young girl, feels as she is faced with the stereotype of a southern lady.

Focus Your Reading

Vocabulary Words to Know

Study the following words and definitions. You will meet these words in your reading. Be sure to jot down in your word journal any other unknown words from the reading.

detachment—indifference; absence of prejudice or bias

tyrannical—having absolute authority

revelation—the act of revealing or disclosing

asylum—an institution for the care of people with physical or mental impairments

entailment—to limit the inheritance of property to a specified succession of heirs; the state of being entailed

contentious—quarrelsome

disapprobation—moral disapproval; condemnation

auspicious—attended by favorable circumstances; favorable

arbitrated—decided in or as in the manner of a judge

edification—intellectual, moral, or spiritual improvement; enlightenment

Things to Know

Here is some background information about this section of the book.

Maycomb, Alabama, is the small southern town where *To Kill a Mockingbird* takes place.

The Gray Ghost is a book written by Seckatary Hawkins. Hawkins is the pseudonym, or pen name, of Robert F. Schulkers.

Meridian, Mississippi, is the town where Dill lives during the school year.

Hookworms are parasites that usually enter the body through bare feet and move through the body to the small intestines. There they attach themselves with a series of hooks around their mouths.

Indian-head pennies are pennies with a picture of an Indian head on the front side. This U. S. one-cent coin was issued from 1859 until 1909. After that, the one-cent coin was issued with the wheat sheaf on the reverse and Lincoln on the front. This penny is called the Wheat Penny.

"Foot-washing Baptist" refers to a religious fanatic, someone who believes that all pleasure is sinful.

Focus Your Reading

Questions to Think About

The following questions will help you understand the meaning of what you read. You do not have to write out the answers to these questions. Instead, look at them before you begin reading, and think about them while you are reading.

1. Why do you think Scout and Jem are friends with Dill? What does Dill bring to the friendship?

2. How is school different in the book for the children of Maycomb County from what it is today? How do different characters in the book feel about education?

3. How do you think Scout feels about Calpurnia?

4. Why are the children so interested in Boo Radley?

5. How do Scout and Jem feel about their father? Do they respect his wishes?

Build Your Vocabulary

Read the sentences below. On the line, write your definition of the word in bold type. Then, on another sheet of paper, use that word in a new sentence of your own.

1. "Jem and I found our father satisfactory: he played with us, read to us, and treated us with courteous **detachment**."
   detachment: _____

2. "She had been with us ever since Jem was born, and I had felt her **tyrannical** presence as long as I could remember."
   tyrannical: _____

3. "Dill had seen *Dracula*, a **revelation** that moved Jem to eye him with the beginning of respect."
   revelation: _____

4. "Miss Stephanie said old Mr. Radley said no Radley was going to any **asylum**, when it was suggested that a season in Tuscaloosa might be helpful to Boo."
   asylum: _____

5. "**Entailment** was only a part of Mr. Cunningham's vexations. The acres not entailed were mortgaged to the hilt. . . ."
   entailment: _____

6. "'Ain't got no mother,' was the answer, 'and their paw's [father's] right **contentious**.'"
   contentious: _____

7. "'Scout, you'd better not say anything about our agreement. . . . I'm afraid our activities would be received with considerable **disapprobation** by the more learned authorities.'"
   disapprobation: _____

8. "The remainder of my schooldays were no more **auspicious** than the first."
   auspicious: _____

9. "Dill said he ought to be first, he just got here. Jem **arbitrated**, awarded me first push with an extra time for Dill, and I folded myself inside the tire."
   arbitrated: _____

10. "'No,' said Atticus, 'putting his life's history on display for the **edification** of the neighborhood.'"
    edification: _____

Check Your Understanding

Multiple Choice

Circle the letter of the best answer to each question.

1. Where do Atticus, Scout, and Jem Finch live?
   a. Maycomb, Alabama
   b. Meridian, Mississippi
   c. Montgomery, Alabama

2. Who is Calpurnia?
   a. a kind neighbor
   b. the Finches' cook
   c. Scout's grade-school teacher

3. What happened to Scout and Jem's mother?
   a. She died of a heart attack.
   b. She's in a mental institution.
   c. She left Maycomb to live with her sister in Montgomery.

4. Who taught Scout how to read?
   a. her father
   b. Miss Maudie
   c. her brother, Jem

5. How do the Ewell children feel about school?
   a. School is a waste of time, and they do not attend.
   b. They attend school just like the other children in the town.
   c. They are home-schooled and learn to read and write from their father.

6. Jem and Scout look forward to summer, to sleeping on the porch and in the tree house. Who do they look forward to spending time with in the summer?
   a. Dill
   b. Uncle Jack
   c. Boo Radley

7. What do Jem and Scout find in the knot-hole of an oak tree at the Radley place?
   a. a silver bell
   b. a prayer book
   c. Indian-head pennies

8. How do Scout and Jem feel about their neighbor, Miss Maudie?
   a. They are afraid of her.
   b. They consider her a friend.
   c. They don't pay much attention to her.

9. What do the children want Boo Radley to do?
   a. to move out of town
   b. to come out of the house
   c. to send the children a letter

10. How does Atticus feel about the children disturbing the Radleys?
    a. He finds it amusing.
    b. He isn't aware of the children's activities.
    c. He wants them to leave the Radleys alone.

Check Your Understanding

Short Answer

Write a short answer for each question.

1. How would you describe Dill's personality? What does he like to do? What type of stories does he tell?

2. How does Miss Caroline react when she learns that Scout already knows how to read?

3. How does Mr. Cunningham pay Atticus Finch for his legal services?

4. How does Burris Ewell behave in school? Does he respect Miss Caroline?

5. How does Calpurnia feel when Scout begins school?

6. What is the first thing that Scout finds in the oak tree on the Radleys' property?

7. Why are Scout and Jem so afraid when Scout gets rolled inside the tire? Where does she end up?

8. Scout, Jem, and Dill entertain themselves by acting out a drama. What story do they act out?

9. How does Miss Maudie show her affection for Scout and Jem?

10. What is Jem, Scout, and Dill's first attempt to communicate with Boo Radley?

Deepen Your Understanding

Mood refers to the climate of feeling, or atmosphere, created by the author. How do the rumors about Boo Radley and his family's history affect the mood? Does the mood help spark your interest in Boo Radley? Are you curious, or frightened? Give specific examples of passages that create the mood from the first five chapters of the book.

Focus Your Reading

Vocabulary Words to Know

Study the following words and definitions. You will meet these words in your reading. Be sure to jot down in your word journal any other unknown words from the reading.

malignant—showing great ill will; evil

desolate—dreary; dismal; sad

provocation—the act of deliberately angering someone

deportment—a manner of personal conduct; behavior

obstreperous—noisily and stubbornly defiant

wrathful—fiercely angry

umbrage—offense; resentment

interdict—to forbid authoritatively

palliation—making something (an offense or a crime) seem less serious

propensities—natural inclinations; tendencies

Things to Know

Here is some background information about this section of the book.

Strip poker is a poker card game in which the losing players in each hand must remove an article of clothing.

The **Rosetta Stone** is a basalt tablet with inscriptions that gave the first clue to the meaning of Egyptian hieroglyphics. It was discovered in 1799 near Rosetta, a town in northern Egypt in the Nile River delta.

The **Missouri Compromise** was an 1820 measure worked out between the North and the South and passed by the U.S. Congress that allowed for admission of Missouri as the 24th state (1821). It marked the beginning of the prolonged sectional conflict over the extension of slavery that, along with other issues, led to the American Civil War.

A **hookah** is an Eastern smoking pipe. It has a long tube passing through an urn of water that cools the smoke as it is drawn through.

An **Add-A-Pearl necklace** is a traditional gift for a young girl that begins with one, three, or five pearls on a 14-karat gold chain. As the years go by, the necklace may grow into a full strand of pearls as friends and family add gifts of pearls.

Focus Your Reading (continued)

Mockingbirds are gray-and-white birds of the southern and eastern United States noted for the ability to mimic the sounds of other birds.

A **Jew's Harp** is a small musical instrument consisting of a lyre-shaped metal frame that is held between the teeth and a projecting steel tongue that is plucked to produce a soft twanging sound.

Morphine is a medication extracted from opium. It is a powerful, habit-forming narcotic used to relieve pain. A morphine addict is physiologically or psychologically dependent on taking the drug.

Questions to Think About

The following questions will help you understand the meaning of what you read. You do not have to write out the answers to these questions. Instead, look at them before you begin reading, and think about them while you are reading.

1. Who plugged up the knot-hole in the oak tree, and why?

2. Why does Scout fight with her cousin Francis, and how does she feel about her Uncle Jack's reaction?

3. How does Scout and Jem's opinion of their father change after he shoots the mad dog?

4. Why does Atticus want Jem to spend time with Mrs. Dubose?

5. Why are Aunt Alexandra and Mrs. Dubose critical of the way Scout dresses and behaves? How do they think she should behave?

Build Your Vocabulary

Read the sentences below. On the line, write your definition of the word in bold type. Then, on another sheet of paper, use that word in a new sentence of your own.

1. "Every night-sound I heard from my cot on the back porch was magnified three-fold; . . . insects splashing against the screen were Boo Radley's insane fingers picking the wire to pieces; the chinaberry trees were **malignant,** hovering, alive."
   malignant: _____

2. "The night-crawlers had retired, but ripe chinaberries drummed on the roof when the wind stirred, and the darkness was **desolate** with the barking of distant dogs."
   desolate: _____

3. "'You like words like damn and hell now, don't you?' I said I reckoned so. 'Well I don't,' said Uncle Jack, 'not unless there's extreme **provocation** connected with 'em. . . .'"
   provocation: _____

4. "Aunt Alexandra's vision of my **deportment** involved playing with small stoves, tea sets, and wearing the Add-A-Pearl necklace she gave me when I was born. . . ."
   deportment: _____

5. "'Such conduct as yours required little understanding. It was **obstreperous,** disorderly and abusive—'"
   obstreperous: _____

6. "If she was on the porch when we passed, we would be raked by her **wrathful** gaze, subjected to ruthless interrogation regarding our behavior, and given a melancholy prediction on what we would amount to when we grew up, which was always nothing."
   wrathful: _____

7. "I wasn't sure what Jem resented most, but I took **umbrage** at Mrs. Dubose's assessment of the family's mental hygiene."
   umbrage: _____

8. "What Jem did was something I'd do as a matter of course had I not been under Atticus's **interdict,** which I assumed included not fighting horrible old ladies."
   interdict: _____

9. "She was a less than satisfactory source of **palliation,** but she did give Jem a hot biscuit-and-butter which he tore in half and shared with me."
   palliation: _____

10. " . . . that is, Mrs. Dubose would hound Jem for a while on her favorite subjects, her camellias and our father's nigger-loving **propensities;** . . ."
    propensities: _____

Check Your Understanding

Multiple Choice

Circle the letter of the best answer to each question.

1. When Jem returned to free his pants from the fence, what did he discover?
   a. The pants were missing.
   b. The pants had been mended.
   c. The pants were cut into ribbons.

2. What do Jem and Scout find in the knot-hole of the oak tree that frightens them?
   a. a knife
   b. a witch figurine
   c. carved figures of a boy and girl

3. What frightens Scout and makes her think the world is coming to an end?
   a. It begins snowing in Maycomb.
   b. The Finches' house catches fire.
   c. She hears gunshots in the night.

4. What does Jem do during the snowstorm?
   a. He goes sledding.
   b. He builds a snowman.
   c. He shovels Miss Maudie's walkway.

5. How do Jem and Scout know Boo Radley came out during Miss Maudie's house fire?
   a. He put a blanket around Scout.
   b. They see his footprints in the snow.
   c. They saw him helping with the fire.

6. Why does Scout stop herself from fighting Cecil Jacobs?
   a. She feels sorry for Cecil.
   b. She is afraid Cecil will hurt her.
   c. Her father has asked her not to fight.

7. Why does Scout break her promise to her father and punch her cousin Francis?
   a. Francis calls Scout's father a nigger-lover.
   b. Francis calls Scout a baby and laughs at her.
   c. Francis makes fun of Dill and calls him a thief.

8. What happens to Harry Johnson's mad dog, Tim Johnson?
   a. Jem shoots him with Atticus's rifle.
   b. Atticus shoots him with Heck Tate's rifle.
   c. He gets sick and dies of a heart attack.

9. What does Jem do out of anger at Mrs. Dubose's insults?
   a. Jem throws Scout's baton through Mrs. Dubose's window.
   b. Jem yells back at Mrs. Dubose and calls her a "horrible old lady."
   c. Jem uses Scout's baton to cut the tops off of Mrs. Dubose's camellias.

10. What does Mrs. Dubose have delivered to Jem after her death?
    a. a camellia
    b. her alarm clock
    c. the book he had been reading to her

Check Your Understanding

Short Answer

Write a short answer for each question.

1. Who sealed up the knot-hole in the oak tree, and why?

2. Why does Scout feel she may be partially responsible for the unusual snowstorm?

3. How does Miss Maudie react when her house burns down?

4. Why does Atticus agree to defend Tom Robinson despite the negative reaction of the townspeople?

5. Why does Scout tell her Uncle Jack that he doesn't understand children?

6. Why do Scout and Jem think of their father as old and weak before the Tom Robinson case?

7. According to Miss Maudie, why is it a sin to kill a mockingbird?

8. Why are Scout and Jem so surprised when Atticus shoots Tim Johnson?

9. Mrs. Dubose criticizes Atticus for two reasons. What are they?

10. Why do Jem and Scout have to read to Mrs. Dubose for longer and longer each day?

Deepen Your Understanding

Discussions about guns appear in several scenes throughout the novel. What does Atticus think about bravery and guns? What does he think about the children's fascination with guns? What does Atticus hope Jem will learn about bravery from spending time with Mrs. Dubose?

Focus Your Reading

Vocabulary Words to Know

Study the following words and definitions. You will meet these words in your reading. Be sure to jot down in your word journal any other unknown words from the reading.

altercation—a loud quarrel

melancholy—sad; depressed; thoughtful

denunciation—a public announcement of disapproval

formidable—inspiring awe, admiration, or wonder

prerogative—an exclusive right or privilege held by a person or group

caste—a social class separated from others by distinctions of hereditary rank, profession, or wealth

futility—uselessness

morbid—psychologically unhealthy

elucidate—to make clear or plain; to clarify

unobtrusive—not noticeable; inconspicuous

Things to Know

Here is some background information about this section of the book.

During the Great Depression, **sit-down strikes** became a real force in labor relations in the United States. These are nonviolent strikes in which protesters sit down at the site of an injustice and refuse to move for a specified period of time or until goals are achieved. A famous example is the Flint (Michigan) sit-down strike of 1936–1937, in which auto workers sat down on the job for forty-four days in protest for union recognition.

Octagon Soap was a harsh lye soap intended primarily for laundry, but often used as an all-purpose soap.

The **Garden of Gethsemane** was where Jesus went to pray on the night before his crucifixion. It was in this garden that he was arrested by Roman soldiers.

Prohibition was the period (1920–1933) during which the 18th Amendment forbidding the manufacture and sale of alcoholic beverages was in force in the United States.

Bootleggers are people who make, sell, and/or transport alcoholic liquor for sale illegally.

The **War Between the States** was the American Civil War (1861–1865).

Focus Your Reading (continued)

Reconstruction was the period of time, roughly between 1867 and 1877, when the Southern states were reorganized and reestablished after the Civil War.

A venue is the locality where a crime is committed or a cause of action occurs. It may also be the locality from which a jury is called and in which a trial is held. In certain cases, the court has power to **change the venue,** which is to direct the trial to be held in a different county from that where the crime was committed.

The **Ku Klux Klan** is a secret society organized in the South after the Civil War to reassert white supremacy by means of terrorism.

Braxton Bragg was the commander of the Western Confederate Army during the Civil War. Bragg led a less-than-distinguished career in the military, and his army unit was eventually defeated.

A **Mennonite** is a member of an Anabaptist church characterized particularly by simplicity of life, pacifism, and nonresistance.

Questions to Think About

The following questions will help you understand the meaning of what you read. You do not have to write out the answers to these questions. Instead, look at them before you begin reading, and think about them while you are reading.

1. Where does Calpurnia take the children, and what do they learn there?

2. How does Aunt Alexandra think Atticus should raise his children? What are her prejudices about class and heredity?

3. Why do Heck Tate and Link Deas come to Atticus's house? What are they concerned about?

4. Why do the men appear outside the Maycomb County jail at night?

5. How does Scout help her father when he is faced with the angry group of men?

III. CHAPTERS 12–16

Build Your Vocabulary

Read the sentences below. On the line, write your definition of the word in bold type. Then, on another sheet of paper, use that word in a new sentence of your own.

1. "After one **altercation** when Jem hollered, ''t's time you started bein' a girl and acting right!' I burst into tears and fled to Calpurnia."
   altercation: _____

2. "Line for line, voices followed in simple harmony until the hymn ended in a **melancholy** murmur."
   melancholy: _____

3. "His sermon was a forthright **denunciation** of sin. . . ."
   denunciation: _____

4. ". . . Aunt Alexandra's was once an hour-glass figure. From any angle, it was **formidable.**"
   formidable: _____

5. "She was never bored, and given the slightest chance she would exercise her royal **prerogative:** she would arrange, advise, caution, and warn."
   prerogative: _____

6. "There was indeed a **caste** system in Maycomb, but to my mind it worked this way: the older citizens, the present generation of people who had lived side by side for years, were utterly predictable to one another. . . ."
   caste: _____

7. "I began to sense the **futility** one feels when unacknowledged by a chance acquaintance."
   futility: _____

8. "''t's **morbid,** watching a poor devil on trial for his life. Look at all those fools, it's like a Roman carnival.'"
   morbid: _____

9. "We asked Miss Maudie to **elucidate:** she said Miss Stephanie seemed to know so much about the case she might as well be called on to testify."
   elucidate: _____

10. "I found myself in the middle of the Idlers' Club and made myself as **unobtrusive** as possible."
    unobtrusive: _____

Check Your Understanding

Multiple Choice

Circle the letter of the best answer to each question.

1. For whom is Reverend Sykes collecting donations at First Purchase Baptist Church?
   a. Calpurnia
   b. Bob Ewell
   c. Helen Robinson

2. What question does Calpurnia tell Scout to ask her father, saying that he can explain it better?
   a. What's rape?
   b. What's a Mennonite?
   c. What's the Ku Klux Klan?

3. What is under Scout's bed?
   a. Dill
   b. a snake
   c. Boo Radley

4. When a group of men appear at the Finches' door to discuss Tom Robinson's trial, what does Jem say to break up the group and avoid trouble for his father?
   a. "Scout needs your help!"
   b. "The telephone's ringing!"
   c. "Calpurnia says it's dinner time."

5. Why does Atticus sit outside the door of the Maycomb County jail?
   a. to prepare for the trial
   b. to wait for Tom Robinson's arrival
   c. to protect Tom Robinson from angry townspeople

6. One of the men in the mob outside the jail at night is Walter Cunningham's father. What does Scout do to keep Mr. Cunningham from harming her father?
   a. She kicks him.
   b. She talks to him kindly.
   c. She tells him about Walter's troubles at school.

7. Who says, "'t's morbid watching a poor devil on trial for his life" and refuses to go to watch Tom Robinson's trial?
   a. Calpurnia
   b. Miss Maudie
   c. Miss Stephanie

8. Where do Scout and Jem sit in the courthouse?
   a. with Atticus and Tom Robinson
   b. in the balcony with the black people
   c. at the back of the courthouse

9. How did Atticus come to represent Tom Robinson in the trial?
   a. Atticus offered to defend Tom Robinson.
   b. Tom requested Atticus Finch as his lawyer.
   c. The court appointed Atticus to defend Tom Robinson.

10. What is Judge Taylor's interesting habit?
    a. He eats constantly during a trial.
    b. He sleeps during the proceedings.
    c. He sometimes chews on an unlit cigar.

Check Your Understanding

Short Answer

Write a short answer for each question.

1. What do Aunt Alexandra and Atticus argue about?

2. What does Jem do when Dill runs away from home and turns up in Scout's bedroom? Why does Scout feel that Jem "broke the remaining code of our childhood"?

3. Dill explains to Scout the real reason he ran away from home. What does he say? How does Scout feel about his reason?

4. Why does Dill think Boo Radley has never tried to run away?

5. Why do Scout and Jem follow Atticus the night he goes to the Maycomb County jail?

6. Scout runs to her father as he faces the group of men outside of the jail. She expects him to be happy to see her, but what is Atticus's reaction?

7. Scout tries to distract the men outside of the jail. What does she talk to Mr. Cunningham about?

8. How does Dill show his respect for Atticus after the scene outside of the jail?

9. After the mob breaks up, is Atticus angry with Jem for disobeying?

10. Jem says, ". . . around here, once you have a drop of Negro blood, that makes you all black." What does he mean by this statement? What issue is he referring to?

Deepen Your Understanding

On two occasions in this part of the novel, Atticus faces a group of angry townspeople. In both cases, the mob breaks up and leaves without incident. Atticus explains to his children that a mob is just made up of people. Mr. Cunningham came to his senses because "you children last night made Walter Cunningham stand in my shoes for a minute. That was enough."

What does Atticus mean about standing in someone's shoes? What does he hope Jem and Scout will learn from this experience about judging or criticizing other people?

Focus Your Reading

Vocabulary Words to Know

Study the following words and definitions. You will meet these words in your reading. Be sure to jot down in your word journal any other unknown words from the reading.

acrimonious—bitter and sharp in language or tone

benignly—showing gentleness and mildness; kindly

complacently—in a self-satisfied and unconcerned manner

articulate—expressing oneself easily in clear and effective language

volition—a conscious choice or decision

collective—made by a number of people acting as a group

predicament—a situation that is difficult to get out of; a dilemma

perpetrate—to be responsible for; to commit

corroborative—supporting (evidence)

temerity—foolhardy disregard of danger; recklessness

Things to Know

Here is some background information about this section of the book.

Before the invention of refrigerators, people used **iceboxes,** large wood cabinets kept cold on the inside by blocks of ice that were delivered to the home.

Model-T Ford (also known as a "tin Lizzie" or a "flivver") was Henry Ford's first popular success. Originally produced in 1909, it was an affordable and relatively reliable automobile.

A **chiffarobe** is a dresser or portable closet with drawers on the side.

A **cotton gin** is a machine used to separate seed and other debris from cotton.

Mr. Jingle is a character in Charles Dickens's novel *The Pickwick Papers*. Mr. Jingle usually expresses himself in sentence fragments.

Ex cathedra remarks are statements made with the authority derived from one's office or position.

The **"distaff side of the Executive branch"** is a reference to Eleanor Roosevelt, the wife of President Franklin D. Roosevelt (the Executive branch is the President, and distaff, in this case, means "wife"). Eleanor Roosevelt was often criticized, especially in the South, for her views on civil rights.

Focus Your Reading (continued)

Albert Einstein (1979–1955) was a German-born American theoretical physicist whose special and general theories of relativity revolutionized modern thought on the nature of space and time and formed a theoretical base for the exploitation of atomic energy.

John D. Rockefeller (1839–1937), one of the richest men in America at the time of the novel, was an oil magnate who amassed great wealth through the Standard Oil Company. He spent about half of his fortune on philanthropic works.

Thomas Jefferson (1743–1826) was the third president of the United States (1801–1809) and an author of The Declaration of Independence.

Questions to Think About

The following questions will help you understand the meaning of what you read. You do not have to write out the answers to these questions. Instead, look at them before you begin reading, and think about them while you are reading.

1. Why does Atticus question Heck Tate so thoroughly about which side of Mayella's face was beaten?

2. Why is Mayella so angry with Atticus when she first takes the witness stand?

3. Why is it impossible for Tom Robinson to have done all of the things Mayella accused him of?

4. Why is it a mistake for Tom Robinson to say that he felt sorry for Mayella?

5. What do the children discover about Mr. Dolphus Raymond and his lifestyle?

Build Your Vocabulary

Read the sentences below. On the line, write your definition of the word in bold type. Then, on another sheet of paper, use that word in a new sentence of your own.

1. "We could tell, however, when debate became more **acrimonious** than professional, but this was from watching lawyers other than our father."
   acrimonious: _____

2. "Judge Taylor stirred. He turned slowly in his swivel chair and looked **benignly** at the witness."
   benignly: _____

3. "Mr. Ewell wrote on the back of the envelope and looked up **complacently** to see Judge Taylor staring at him as if he were some fragrant gardenia in full bloom on the witness stand. . . ."
   complacently: _____

4. "Suddenly Mayella became **articulate.** 'I got somethin' to say,' she said."
   articulate: _____

5. "He seemed to be a respectable Negro, and a respectable Negro would never go up into somebody's yard of his own **volition.**"
   volition: _____

6. "Below us, the spectators drew a **collective** breath and leaned forward. Behind us, the Negroes did the same."
   collective: _____

7. "Until my father explained it to me later, I did not understand the subtlety of Tom's **predicament:** he would not have dared strike a white woman under any circumstances and expect to live long. . . ."
   predicament: _____

8. "I had never encountered a being who deliberately **perpetrated** fraud against himself."
   perpetrated: _____

9. "'. . . absence of any **corroborative** evidence, this man was indicted on a capital charge and is now on trial for his life. . . .'"
   corroborative: _____

10. "'And so a quiet, respectable, humble Negro who had the unmitigated **temerity** to "feel sorry" for a white woman has had to put his word against two white people's.'"
    temerity: _____

Check Your Understanding

Multiple Choice

Circle the letter of the best answer to each question.

1. Where in Maycomb does the Bob Ewell family live?
   a. next to the town cemetery
   b. behind the town garbage dump
   c. across from the county courthouse

2. How does Atticus prove that Bob Ewell is left-handed?
   a. He throws a ball to Mr. Ewell.
   b. He asks Mr. Ewell to write his name.
   c. He asks Mayella under oath whether her father is left-handed.

3. What makes Mayella think that Atticus is making fun of her?
   a. He shakes her hand.
   b. He calls her Miss Mayella.
   c. He takes notes during her testimony.

4. Who, from the courtroom audience, speaks out in support of Tom Robinson's character?
   a. Scout
   b. Link Deas
   c. Mr. Gilmer

5. How does Dill react during Mr. Gilmer's cross-examination of Tom Robinson?
   a. He cries.
   b. He falls asleep.
   c. He shouts out in anger.

6. What does Mr. Dolphus Raymond give Dill to settle his stomach?
   a. whiskey
   b. Coca-Cola
   c. cough syrup

7. What does Atticus do halfway through his closing statement that shocks Jem and Scout?
   a. Atticus removes his coat.
   b. Atticus wipes away a tear from his eye.
   c. Atticus puts his hands on Tom's shoulders.

8. According to Atticus in his closing statement, in which human institution are "all men created equal"?
   a. a court
   b. a church
   c. a school

9. How does Atticus discover that his children are in the courtroom?
   a. Mr. Underwood tells him.
   b. Scout runs to her father during a recess.
   c. Atticus spots them in the balcony during his closing statement.

10. What does Reverend Sykes tell Scout to do as her father exits the courtroom at the close of the trial?
    a. applaud
    b. stand up
    c. follow him

Check Your Understanding

Short Answer

Write a short answer for each question.

1. What is the one beautiful thing on the Ewells' property that seems out of place?

2. According to Mr. Ewell's testimony, why didn't he call a doctor for Mayella?

3. Despite Mayella's testimony, who do you think really beat up Mayella, and why?

4. What is Judge Taylor's unusual habit? Why is Dill impressed with Judge Taylor?

5. Why does Scout feel that Mayella Ewell "must have been the loneliest person in the world"?

6. Why is Dill so upset with Mr. Gilmer's cross-examination of Tom Robinson?

7. Why does Dolphus Raymond pretend to be an alcoholic?

8. What does Atticus say motivated Mayella to accuse Tom Robinson of rape?

9. Atticus states that Tom Robinson's accusers subscribe to an evil assumption. What is that assumption?

10. Scout seems to have a premonition about Tom's fate as she waits in the courtroom. How does Scout describe the atmosphere of the courtroom just before the verdict is read?

Deepen Your Understanding

Through the voice of Scout, Harper Lee uses imagery to depict the character of Bob Ewell in the courtroom. When Mr. Ewell first takes the stand, she says, "a little bantam cock of a man rose and strutted to the stand, the back of his neck reddening at the sound of his name."

Can you find other instances in this part of the novel where Mr. Ewell is described as a rooster? How do Harper Lee's descriptions of Bob Ewell make you feel about the man?

Focus Your Reading

Vocabulary Words to Know

Study the following words and definitions. You will meet these words in your reading. Be sure to jot down in your word journal any other unknown words from the reading.

impassive—revealing no emotion; expressionless

credibility—believability

statute—a law enacted by a legislature

vehement—characterized by forcefulness of expression or intensity of emotion

sordid—morally degraded

apprehension—fearful or uneasy anticipation of the future

impertinence—disrespectfulness

brevity—the quality of being brief in duration; concise

demise—death; the end of existence

recluse—a person who withdraws from the world to live in seclusion

Things to Know

Here is some background information about this section of the book.

Mrunas are a tribe in Africa. At one of Aunt Alexandra's missionary society meetings, Mrs. Merriweather describes how sorry she feels for these people and how J. Grimes Everett is the only one who will help the Mrunas.

Birmingham is a city in Central Alabama.

Mrs. Roosevelt refers to First Lady **Eleanor Roosevelt** (1884–1962), wife of President Franklin D. Roosevelt. The reference **"tryin' to sit with 'em"** in the novel refers to the 1939 incident in which Eleanor Roosevelt attended a meeting for the Southern Conference for Human Welfare in Birmingham, Alabama. She defied state authorities by sitting in the center aisle, between whites and blacks, after police told her she was violating segregation laws by sitting with black people.

A **roly-poly** is also called a pill bug, or any small beetle of the genus Byrrhus, having a rounded body, with the head concealed beneath the thorax allowing it to roll into a ball.

Adolf Hitler (1889–1945) was the Nazi dictator of Germany from 1933 to 1945.

A **holy-roller** is a member of a small religious sect that expresses devotion by shouting and moving around during worship services.

Focus Your Reading (continued)

Uncle Natchell was the cartoon mascot for a fertilizer product called Natural Chilean Nitrate of Soda. Many of the advertisements for this product were in comic strip or story form. In the novel, Little Chuck Little thinks one of these advertising "stories" is an actual current event.

Elmer Davis was a journalist and CBS radio commentator who went on to head the Office of War Information.

Questions to Think About

The following questions will help you understand the meaning of what you read. You do not have to write out the answers to these questions. Instead, look at them before you begin reading, and think about them while you are reading.

1. Why did Judge Taylor choose Atticus to defend Tom Robinson?

2. Why is Atticus so understanding when Bob Ewell threatens him and spits in his face?

3. What is Jem's reasoning for believing that the court system should do away with juries?

4. What is Jem's theory about why the Finches, the Cunninghams, the Ewells, and the Robinsons are different?

5. Why does Scout say she feels more at home in her father's world than in Aunt Alexandra's?

Build Your Vocabulary

Read the sentences below. On the line, write your definition of the word in bold type. Then, on another sheet of paper, use that word in a new sentence of your own.

1. "Atticus was standing under the street light looking as though nothing had happened: his vest was buttoned, his collar and tie were neatly in place, his watch-chain glistened, he was his **impassive** self again."
   impassive: _____

2. "'I destroyed his last shred of **credibility** at that trial, if he had any to begin with.'"
   credibility: _____

3. "He said he didn't have any quarrel with the rape **statute,** none whatever, but he did have deep misgivings when the state asked for and the jury gave a death penalty on purely circumstantial evidence."
   statute: _____

4. "I looked up, and his face was **vehement.** 'There's nothing more sickening to me than a low-grade white man who'll take advantage of a Negro's ignorance.'"
   vehement: _____

5. "'I guess it's to protect our frail ladies from **sordid** cases like Tom's.'"
   sordid: _____

6. "Rather nervous, I took a seat beside Miss Maudie. . . . Ladies in bunches always filled me with vague **apprehension** and a firm desire to be elsewhere. . . .'"
   apprehension: _____

7. "Miss Stephanie eyed me suspiciously, decided that I meant no **impertinence,** and contented herself with, 'Well, you won't get very far until you start wearing dresses more often.'"
   impertinence: _____

8. "'I'm sure you do,' Miss Maudie said shortly. . . . When Miss Maudie was angry her **brevity** was icy."
   brevity: _____

9. "Maycomb had lost no time in getting Mr. Ewell's views of Tom's **demise** and passing them along through that English Channel of gossip, Miss Stephanie Crawford."
   demise: _____

10. "I sometimes felt a twinge of remorse, when passing by the old place, at ever having taken part in what must have been sheer torment to Arthur Radley—what reasonable **recluse** wants children peeping through his shutters. . . .'"
    recluse: _____

Check Your Understanding

Multiple Choice

Circle the letter of the best answer to each question.

1. When Bob Ewell accused Atticus of being too proud to fight, how did Atticus respond?
   a. Atticus said he was too old to fight.
   b. Atticus walked away without saying a word.
   c. Atticus pushed Mr. Ewell aside and walked away.

2. Why can't Miss Maudie serve on the jury if she wants to?
   a. She is too old.
   b. She is a woman.
   c. She lives in the same county as Tom Robinson.

3. According to Atticus, who is the one person on the jury who had trouble agreeing to the guilty verdict?
   a. Link Deas
   b. Dolphus Raymond
   c. Walter Cunningham

4. Why does Aunt Alexandra say that Scout cannot invite Walter Cunningham over?
   a. He is trash.
   b. He is too dirty.
   c. He is too old for her to play with.

5. Jem thinks he has discovered why Boo Radley never comes out of his house. What is Jem's reason?
   a. Boo Radley is insane.
   b. Boo Radley wants to stay inside.
   c. Boo Radley's father makes him stay inside.

6. Why is Mrs. Merriweather concerned that the "cooks and field hands are dissatisfied" about Tom Robinson's conviction?
   a. She feels that the verdict was unfair.
   b. She finds it annoying to deal with unhappy servants.
   c. She thinks they will no longer work for white people.

7. How does Tom Robinson die?
   a. He starves himself.
   b. Another prison inmate stabs Tom.
   c. He is shot and killed trying to escape.

8. How does Helen Robinson react when Atticus comes to tell her the news of her husband's death?
   a. She collapses into the dirt.
   b. She runs screaming into a field.
   c. She turns her back on Atticus.

9. In Scout's class at school, what topic leads to a discussion of democracy?
   a. Tom Robinson's trial
   b. sit-down strikes in Birmingham
   c. Hitler and his persecution of the Jews

10. According to Atticus, why is Jem not acting like himself?
    a. He is dealing with his feelings about the trial.
    b. Jem is interested in girls.
    c. Jem is anxious about gaining weight for football.

Check Your Understanding

Short Answer

Write a short answer for each question.

1. How does the black community feel about Atticus after Tom Robinson is convicted?

2. Why does Miss Maudie make a small cake for Scout and Dill but give Jem a piece from a large cake?

3. What does Dill say he wants to be when he grows up?

4. How did Bob Ewell react to Atticus when he ran into him after the trial?

5. How does Atticus finally realize how frightened his children are about Mr. Ewell's threats?

6. Why is it significant that the jury took a few hours instead of a few minutes to reach a verdict?

7. What does Scout tell Mrs. Merriweather she wants to be when she grows up?

8. In the *Maycomb Tribune,* to what does Mr. Underwood compare Tom's death?

9. Scout is reminded of Arthur Radley as a person when she thinks about the things he left in the tree: the Indian-head pennies, the soap dolls, and so on. What is her fantasy surrounding Boo Radley?

10. What troubles Scout about her teacher, Miss Gates's, condemnation of prejudice?

Deepen Your Understanding

In Chapter 24, Aunt Alexandra hosts a missionary society meeting. Here the women discuss the Mrunas of Africa and the work being done to "help" them. The women feel sorry for the people of this far away African tribe, and Mrs. Merriweather says of the Mrunas, "Not a white person'll go near 'em but that saintly J. Grimes Everett."

How does the women's concern for the Mrunas compare to their attitude toward the black people of Maycomb county? Why do you think Harper Lee introduces the missionary society meeting to the novel? Does the portrayal of Mrs. Merriweather and Mrs. Farrow help the reader understand the prejudice of the time?

Focus Your Reading

Vocabulary Words to Know

Study the following words and definitions. You will meet these words in your reading. Be sure to jot down in your word journal any other unknown words from the reading.

purloined—stole, often in a violation of trust

ascertain—to discover with certainty

reeling—thrown off balance and falling

instinctive—arising from a natural impulse; spontaneous and unthinking

turmoil—extreme upset

garishly—glaringly; dazzlingly

audible—able to be heard

disengaged—pulled back; released from something binding

amiable—friendly

acquiescence—passive agreement

Things to Know

Here is some background information about this section of the book.

When millions of Americans were out of work during the Great Depression, the government instituted the Works Progress Administration, or **WPA,** and employed over eight million people.

The **Ladies' Law,** from the Criminal Code of Alabama, Vol. III, 1907, reads: "Any person who enters into, or goes sufficiently near to the dwelling house of another, and, in the presence or hearing of the family of the occupant thereof, or any member of his family, or any person who, in the presence or hearing of any girl or woman, uses abusive, insulting or obscene language must, on conviction, be fined not more than two hundred dollars, and may also be imprisoned in the county jail, or sentenced to hard labour for the county for not more than six months."

National Recovery Act (NRA) was a series of programs set up to help the nation, especially the nation's businesses, recover from the effects of the Great Depression. It was ruled unconstitutional by the Supreme Court in 1935. "NRA—We do our part" was the motto of the NRA.

"Nine old men" is a reference to the nine members of the Supreme Court.

Focus Your Reading

Questions to Think About

The following questions will help you understand the meaning of what you read. You do not have to write out the answers to these questions. Instead, look at them before you begin reading, and think about them while you are reading.

1. What events occur in Maycomb during this part of the novel that make Bob Ewell look suspicious?

2. What causes the Maycomb ladies to organize a Halloween festival and Mrs. Merriweather to write a pageant?

3. What happens to Scout and Jem on their way home from the pageant?

4. Why does the Sheriff insist that Mr. Ewell killed himself by falling on the knife? Who is Mr. Tate trying to protect?

5. Why does Scout feel sad when Boo returns to his home?

Build Your Vocabulary

Read the sentences below. On the line, write your definition of the word in bold type. Then, on another sheet of paper, use that word in a new sentence of your own.

1. "Miss Tutti was sure those traveling fur sellers who came through town two days ago had **purloined** their furniture."
   purloined: _____

2. "After consulting a tree to **ascertain** from its lichen which way was south, and taking no lip from the subordinates who ventured to correct him . . ."
   ascertain: _____

3. "I took one giant step and found myself **reeling:** my arms useless, in the dark, I could not keep my balance."
   reeling: _____

4. "For once in his life, Atticus's **instinctive** courtesy failed him: he sat where he was."
   instinctive: _____

5. "His age was beginning to show, his one sign of inner **turmoil,** the strong line of his jaw melted a little, one became aware of telltale creases forming under his ears. . . ."
   turmoil: _____

6. "They were white hands, sickly white hands that had never seen the sun, so white they stood out **garishly** against the dull cream wall in the dim light of Jem's room."
   garishly: _____

7. "When Mr. Tate spoke again his voice was barely **audible.**"
   audible: _____

8. "I ran to him and hugged him and kissed him with all my might. . . . Atticus **disengaged** himself and looked at me."
   disengaged: _____

9. "'Well, I think I'll stay with you for a while.' 'Suit yourself,' said Atticus. It must have been after midnight, and I was puzzled by his **amiable acquiescence.**"
   amiable: _____
   acquiescence: _____

Check Your Understanding

Multiple Choice

Circle the letter of the best answer to each question.

1. What is Scout's costume for the Halloween pageant?
   a. a cow
   b. a ham
   c. a sheep

2. How much money does Jem give Scout to spend at the Halloween festival?
   a. five cents
   b. thirty cents
   c. two dollars

3. What happens to Scout when it is her turn to come on stage during the pageant?
   a. She trips and falls off the stage.
   b. She falls asleep and misses her cue.
   c. She gets stage fright and refuses to come on.

4. Who do Jem and Scout think is following them home after the pageant?
   a. Arthur Radley
   b. Mrs. Maudie
   c. Cecil Jacobs

5. In the dark, how does Scout know that they are under the big oak tree?
   a. She hears the wind rustle the leaves.
   b. The ground feels colder under her feet.
   c. Her hands brush the knot-hole in the tree.

6. Who asks to leave the room after hearing about Bob Ewell's death?
   a. Scout Finch
   b. Atticus Finch
   c. Aunt Alexandra

7. What is the first thing that Scout says to Arthur Radley when she sees him in her house?
   a. "Hey, Boo."
   b. "Who are you?"
   c. "Thank you for saving us."

8. Where does Atticus lead Scout and Arthur Radley to talk after Dr. Reynolds arrives?
   a. the kitchen
   b. the living room
   c. the front porch

9. After checking to see how Jem is doing, what does Boo ask of Scout?
   a. to walk him home
   b. to give Jem a book
   c. not to tell anyone about him

10. What does Atticus read to Scout the night of Bob Ewell's attack?
    a. the Bible
    b. *The Gray Ghost*
    c. *the Maycomb Tribune*

Check Your Understanding

Short Answer

Write a short answer for each question.

1. What happens to Helen Robinson, and who comes to her assistance?

2. Why is it important that Scout is wearing her Halloween costume during the attack by Bob Ewell?

3. What happens to Bob Ewell, and who is responsible?

4. Why is Scout so surprised when Dr. Reynolds greets Arthur Radley casually?

5. Why does Atticus suggest that Scout, Boo, and Mr. Tate talk out on the front porch rather than in the living room?

6. Why is Atticus hesitant to go along with Heck Tate's cover-up of Bob Ewell's death?

7. How does Scout explain to her father that she understands why it is necessary to cover up the truth about Bob Ewell's death?

8. When Scout brings Boo Radley to Jem's bedside, what does she sense that Boo would like to do?

9. What does Scout feel she's given Boo Radley? Why is she sad when he returns home?

10. Why does Scout want Atticus to read *The Gray Ghost* to her?

Deepen Your Understanding

Authors often use a literary device called foreshadowing in their writing to suggest or hint at an event in the plot before it occurs. In *To Kill a Mockingbird*, how does Harper Lee foreshadow Bob Ewell's attack on the children and Boo Radley's goodness?

What earlier events lead up to the climactic scene on Halloween night?

End-of-Book Test

Circle the letter of the best answer to each question.

1. What did Boo Radley once do that resulted in the sheriff locking him in the courthouse basement?
   a. He broke into Judge Taylor's home.
   b. He stabbed his father with scissors.
   c. He broke the windows in the town hall.

2. How does Scout gain her special knowledge of the Cunninghams?
   a. Mr. Cunningham is Atticus's client.
   b. Mr. Cunningham works with Atticus.
   c. Scout has always played with Walter Cunningham, Jr.

3. What is Scout, Jem, and Dill's favorite pastime during the summer?
   a. swimming in the creek
   b. reading books in the tree house
   c. play-acting the Boo Radley stories

4. What does Jem want to be one day?
   a. a lawyer
   b. a teacher
   c. a football player

5. What happens the night Jem and Dill attempt to peek in Boo's window?
   a. Nathan Radley shoots at them.
   b. Boo Radley runs after them but can't catch them.
   c. Atticus stops them before they reach the Radleys' fence.

6. According to Nathan Radley, why did he fill the knot-hole in the oak tree?
   a. The tree was dying.
   b. He didn't want the children climbing the tree.
   c. He didn't want animals to nest there.

7. What fearful event awakens the town of Maycomb during the middle of the night?
   a. Miss Maudie's house is on fire.
   b. Lightning sets fire to the Maycomb County Courthouse.
   c. Miss Stephanie calls the sheriff because someone is breaking into her house.

8. Why is Uncle Jack so angry with Scout when she visits Aunt Alexandra?
   a. She lies to him.
   b. She uses bad language.
   c. She is disrespectful to Aunt Alexandra.

9. Why does Jem become so angry with Mrs. Dubose that he destroys her garden?
   a. She said that Jem and Scout were trash.
   b. She said that Calpurnia could not be trusted.
   c. She criticized Jem's father for defending a black man.

10. What does Reverend Sykes do when the congregation does not donate enough money for Helen Robinson?
    a. He donates the needed amount himself.
    b. He says that there would be no church service until the necessary amount is raised.
    c. He locks the doors of the church and won't let anyone leave until enough money is raised.

(continued)

End-of-Book Test (continued)

11. According to Atticus, who will never come back to Maycomb?
    a. Aunt Alexandra
    b. Roman Catholics
    c. the Ku Klux Klan

12. Why is Scout surprised that Mr. Cunningham is one of the men who threatens Atticus outside the jail?
    a. She thought he was a friend.
    b. She thought he was a coward.
    c. She thought he supported Tom Robinson.

13. Why did Mayella really ask Tom Robinson to come into the house?
    a. She wanted to make her father angry.
    b. She was attracted to him and wanted his attention.
    c. She wanted him to chop up a dresser to use for firewood.

14. Why does Scout have to leave during Mr. Gilmer's cross-examination of Tom Robinson?
    a. She feels sick and wants to leave the courtroom.
    b. She leaves with Dill because he can't stop crying.
    c. Jem makes her leave because the trial is not appropriate for her to watch.

15. Aunt Alexandra thinks that background and gentle breeding determine social class. What does Jem think determines class?
    a. money
    b. education
    c. kindness

16. Why is Scout impressed with Aunt Alexandra after hearing about Tom Robinson's death?
    a. She cancels the missionary society meeting and asks everyone to leave.
    b. She continues to be a gracious hostess at the missionary society meeting.
    c. She goes with Atticus to tell Helen Robinson the news of her husband's death.

17. What current event discussed in school leads Scout to wonder how people can "be ugly about folks right at home"?
    a. poverty and breadlines
    b. labor strikes in Michigan
    c. Adolf Hitler's dictatorship

18. How does Helen Robinson support her family after Tom's death?
    a. She goes on welfare.
    b. She works as a cook.
    c. She moves in with her sister's family.

19. How does Scout react when she sees Boo Radley for the first time?
    a. She runs and hugs him.
    b. She speaks to him kindly.
    c. She cries and runs to Atticus.

20. How did Bob Ewell really die?
    a. Atticus shot him with his shotgun in self-defense.
    b. Link Deas shot him with his rifle to protect Helen Robinson.
    c. Arthur Radley stabbed him with a knife to protect Jem and Scout.

I. Chapters 1–5

Build Your Vocabulary

Wording of definitions may vary. Students may remember the definitions given in the Vocabulary Words to Know section of Focus Your Reading, or they may refine the definition based on the context of the sentence and the reading overall. Students' new sentences will vary.

Check Your Understanding: Multiple Choice

1. a
2. b
3. a
4. a
5. a
6. a
7. c
8. b
9. b
10. c

Check Your Understanding: Short Answer

1. Dill is adventurous and likes to tell fantastic stories. His stories are imaginative, and Jem and Scout have trouble believing many of them.
2. Miss Caroline is angry that Scout has already learned to read and feels that learning at home will interfere with her learning to read properly.
3. He has little money, so he pays Atticus in goods such as firewood and nuts.
4. Burris Ewell despises Miss Caroline and feels that school is a waste of time. He only attends the first day of every year.
5. Calpurnia misses Scout's company when she goes to school. Calpurnia bakes cracklin' bread for Scout and kisses her when she comes home.
6. two sticks of chewing gum
7. Scout rolls out of control and ends up at the foot of the Radleys' front steps.
8. They act out the legendary story of Arthur Radley stabbing his father with scissors.
9. She talks to them as friends and bakes cakes for them to take home to their father.
10. They attach a note to the end of a fishing pole and attempt to stick it through the shutters of the Radleys' front window.

Deepen Your Understanding

Answers will vary.

II. Chapters 6–11

Build Your Vocabulary

Wording of definitions may vary. Students may remember the definitions given in the Vocabulary Words to Know section of Focus Your Reading, or they may refine the definition based on the context of the sentence and the reading overall. Students' new sentences will vary.

Check Your Understanding: Multiple Choice

1. b
2. c
3. a
4. b
5. a
6. c
7. a
8. b
9. c
10. a

Check Your Understanding: Short Answer

1. Mr. Radley filled the knot-hole with cement to stop Boo from leaving things for Scout and Jem.
2. Mr. Avery says that when children disobey their parents, the season will change, and Scout feels guilty for disobeying her father and bothering the Radleys.
3. She has a positive attitude and says she always wanted a smaller house to have more space for her gardens.
4. Atticus feels it is his duty as a lawyer, as a member of the town, and as a father to give the man a fair trial.
5. Uncle Jack doesn't ask Scout to explain her side of the story before punishing her for hitting Francis.
6. Atticus is almost fifty, older than many of the other parents. He works in an office, doesn't hunt or play poker, and is almost blind in one eye.
7. Miss Maudie says, "Mockingbirds don't do one thing but make music for us to enjoy."
8. They didn't know he had a talent for shooting a gun and that his nickname was One Shot when he was a boy. Scout and Jem thought they knew everything about their father.
9. She thinks that Atticus lets his children run wild, and she disapproves of him helping or lawyering for a black person.

10. Mrs. Dubose is trying to break a morphine addiction before she dies, and listening to the story is a distraction.

Deepen Your Understanding
Answers will vary.

III. CHAPTERS 12–16

Build Your Vocabulary
Wording of definitions may vary. Students may remember the definitions given in the Vocabulary Words to Know section of Focus Your Reading, or they may refine the definition based on the context of the sentence and the reading overall. Students' new sentences will vary.

Check Your Understanding: Multiple Choice
1. c	6. b
2. a	7. b
3. a	8. b
4. b	9. c
5. c	10. c

Check Your Understanding: Short Answer
1. Alexandra disagrees with the way Atticus is raising his children, and she feels that Calpurnia is not needed. She feels that Scout and Jem should live up to their name and their "gentle breeding."
2. Jem tells Atticus that Dill is there. He acts maturely and feels it is wrong to let Dill's mother worry about him any longer. In this instance, Dill takes the perspective of an adult rather than a child.
3. Dill explains that his mother and step-father are not mean to him. They buy him things and care for him, but he feels that they don't really want him around. Dill says that "they do get along a lot better without me." Scout feels needed and wanted by Jem, Atticus, and Calpurnia. She has trouble understanding how Dill's parents could not need him.
4. Unlike Dill, who has his Aunt Rachel and the Finches in Maycomb County, Boo Radley may not have anywhere else to go or anyone else to help him.
5. Scout and Jem are curious because Atticus takes an extension cord with a light on one end and

says he's going out for a while. Jem feels uneasy and says, "I've just got this feeling."
6. Atticus is frightened for his children's safety and tells them to go home.
7. Scout tries to think of topics that would interest Mr. Cunningham. She talks about his son Walter and the family's entailment.
8. He offers to carry the chair home for him.
9. No, Atticus doesn't seem angry. He tousles Jem's hair, which Scout says is Atticus's "one gesture of affection."
10. Jem refers to children with parents of two different races. They have trouble fitting in or being accepted by either race.

Deepen Your Understanding
Answers will vary.

IV. CHAPTERS 17–21

Build Your Vocabulary
Wording of definitions may vary. Students may remember the definitions given in the Vocabulary Words to Know section of Focus Your Reading, or they may refine the definition based on the context of the sentence and the reading overall. Students' new sentences will vary.

Check Your Understanding: Multiple Choice
1. b	6. b
2. b	7. a
3. b	8. a
4. b	9. a
5. a	10. b

Check Your Understanding: Short Answer
1. jars of carefully grown, brilliant red geraniums, thought to be Mayella's
2. He says he had never called a doctor in his life, and it would have cost him five dollars.
3. Her father beat her because he was furious that she made advances or was looking for attention from Tom Robinson.
4. Judge Taylor doesn't smoke a cigar, but he chews on it. Dill is impressed with the judge's aim when he spits into the spittoon.
5. She has no friends. White people think of her family as trash, and black people don't want anything to do with her because she is white.

6. He thinks it is sickening the way Mr. Gilmer talks to Tom, calling him "boy" and sneering. Atticus did not talk that way to Mr. Ewell or Mayella.

7. He does this so that people can blame his alcoholism for the way he lives. Dolphus doesn't want to change, and he doesn't want people to pressure him to do so.

8. Mayella acted out of guilt. Her desire for Tom Robinson was socially unacceptable, and the only way for her to hide her disgrace was to accuse him of taking her against her will.

9. The assumption is "that all Negroes lie, that all Negroes are basically immoral beings, that all Negro men are not to be trusted with our women."

10. She feels as if the courtroom is a cold, "deserted, waiting, empty street," even though it is filled with people.

Deepen Your Understanding

Answers will vary.

V. CHAPTERS 22–26

Build Your Vocabulary

Wording of definitions may vary. Students may remember the definitions given in the Vocabulary Words to Know section of Focus Your Reading, or they may refine the definition based on the context of the sentence and the reading overall. Students' new sentences will vary.

Check Your Understanding: Multiple Choice

1. a	6. b
2. b	7. c
3. c	8. a
4. a	9. c
5. b	10. a

Check Your Understanding: Short Answer

1. The black community shows its support and respect for Atticus by bringing generous amounts of food to his house.

2. She acknowledges that Jem is more grown-up than the other two children.

3. He says that he can't do anything about the way people act, so he wants to be a clown who laughs at people.

4. Mr. Ewell spits in Atticus's face and tells him that he will get even with him.

5. He notices that they aren't eating and show little interest in their usual activities.

6. The fact that the jury deliberated at all is a positive sign for race equality. Atticus sees this as a beginning.

7. She doesn't know how to respond and says simply, "Just a lady."

8. He likens Tom's death to the senseless slaughter of songbirds (mockingbirds).

9. She imagines talking with him just as she would with any friendly neighbor.

10. She overhears Miss Gates make discriminating remarks against blacks, yet the teacher feels it is wrong of Hitler to persecute the Jews. Scout realizes that Miss Gates is a hypocrite.

Deepen Your Understanding

Answers will vary. You may want to introduce the literary term *irony* and discuss how Harper Lee includes the missionary society meeting as a contrast to the women's attitudes toward the black citizens of Maycomb.

VI. CHAPTERS 27–31

Build Your Vocabulary

Wording of definitions may vary. Students may remember the definitions given in the Vocabulary Words to Know section of Focus Your Reading, or they may refine the definition based on the context of the sentence and the reading overall. Students' new sentences will vary.

Check Your Understanding: Multiple Choice

1. b	6. c
2. b	7. a
3. b	8. c
4. c	9. a
5. b	10. b

Check Your Understanding: Short Answer

1. Bob Ewell harasses and frightens Helen on her way to work, and Link Deas comes to her defense.

2. The chicken wire of the costume protects Scout from Mr. Ewell's attack, but it also hinders her ability to see what is going on.

3. Boo Radley stabs Mr. Ewell in the chest with a kitchen knife to save Scout and Jem.

4. It seems as if Dr. Reynolds knows Arthur well, and Scout realizes that even Arthur Radley may need to see the doctor occasionally.

5. Atticus senses that Boo Radley would be more comfortable on the dimly lit porch than under the bright lights of the living room.

6. Atticus is afraid that lying will threaten his integrity with his children, and he doesn't want to lose their respect or trust.

7. Scout says that telling the truth would be like "shootin' a mockingbird."

8. Scout starts to sense Boo's body language and knows that he would like to touch Jem.

9. Scout feels that Boo has given her and Jem so much and that they have given him nothing. She feels sad that she has never given in return.

10. The plot of the story reminds her of Boo Radley because people misunderstand a character in the book and realize at the end that they were wrong about him.

Deepen Your Understanding

Answers will vary. Answers may include Bob Ewell's threats against Atticus after the trial, as well as his suspicious behavior toward the judge and Helen Robinson, foreshadow his attack on the children; Aunt Alexandra's premonition and the ominous dark night of Halloween creates tension leading to the attack; the presents Jem and Scout find in the oak tree, the mended pants, and the blanket for Scout foreshadow the eventual discovery of Boo Radley's goodness.

END-OF-BOOK TEST

1. b	11. c
2. a	12. a
3. c	13. b
4. a	14. b
5. a	15. b
6. a	16. b
7. a	17. c
8. b	18. b
9. c	19. b
10. c	20. c

SADDLEBACK
EDUCATIONAL PUBLISHING

MORE EXCITING TITLES

SADDLEBACK'S "IN CONTEXT" SERIES
(Six 112-page worktexts in each series)
- English
- Vocabulary
- Reading
- Practical Math

SADDLEBACK'S "SKILLS AND STRATEGIES" SERIES
(Six 144-page reproducible workbooks in each series)
- Building Vocabulary
- Language Arts
- Math Computation
- Reading Comprehension

READING COMPREHENSION SKILL BOOSTERS
- Read-Reflect-Respond, Books A, B, C, & D

WRITING 4
(Four 64-page worktexts)
- Descriptive Writing
- Expository Writing
- Narrative Writing
- Persuasive Writing

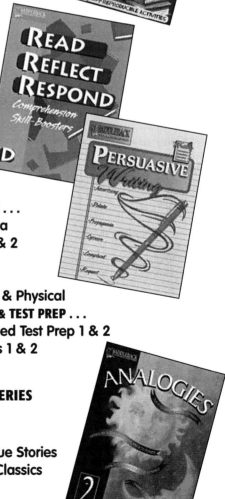

CURRICULUM BINDERS
(100+ activities in each binder)

ENGLISH, READING, WRITING . . .
- Beginning Writing 1 & 2
- Writing 1 & 2
- Good Grammar
- Language Arts 1 & 2
- Reading for Information 1 & 2
- Reading Comprehension 1 & 2
- Spelling Steps 1, 2, 3, & 4
- Survival Vocabulary 1 & 2

MATHEMATICS . . .
- Pre-Algebra
- Algebra 1 & 2
- Geometry

SCIENCE . . .
- Earth, Life, & Physical

STUDY SKILLS & TEST PREP . . .
- Standardized Test Prep 1 & 2
- Study Skills 1 & 2

SADDLEBACK'S HIGH-INTEREST READING SERIES
- Astonishing Headlines
- Barclay Family Adventures
- Carter High
- Disasters
- Illustrated Classics Series
- Life of…Series
- PageTurners
- Quickreads
- Strange But True Stories
- Saddleback's Classics
- Walker High

Visit us at www.sdlback.com for even more Saddleback titles.